CARVER

RUTH YAFFE RADIN

CARVER

ILLUSTRATED BY KARL SWANSON

MACMILLAN PUBLISHING COMPANY
NEW YORK

COLLIER MACMILLAN PUBLISHERS
LONDON

Macmillan Publishing Company
866 Third Avenue, New York, NY 10022
Collier Macmillan Canada, Inc.
First Edition   Printed in the United States of America

10   9   8   7   6   5   4   3   2   1

The text of this book is set in 12 point Goudy Old Style.
The illustrations are rendered in pencil on paper.
Library of Congress Cataloging-in-Publication Data
Radin, Ruth Yaffe. Carver / Ruth Yaffe Radin :
illustrated by Karl Swanson.
-- 1st American ed.   p.   cm.
Summary: Blind and fatherless since the age of two, ten-year-
old Jon struggles to fit in at his new public school and hide his
growing interest in wood carving from his mom who still
mourns the death of Jon's father who hoped to become a
professional wood carver.
ISBN 0-02-775651-3
[1. Blind--Fiction. 2. Physically handicapped--
Fiction. 3. Wood carving--Fiction.]
I. Swanson, Karl W., ill.   II. Title.
PZ7.R1216Car   1990   [Fic]--dc20
89-13413 CIP AC

In memory of

CURTIS MERRITT

ONE

JON FACED THE BAY. He could hear the baseball game being played behind him on the other side of the low wooden fence, but he didn't pay much attention to it until he heard a ball land near him.

"Could you throw it back to me?" a boy shouted.

"Where is it?" Jon yelled as he turned around.

"What's the matter? Are you blind?"

"Yeah!"

There was a pause and then Jon heard the sound of someone running, then stopping about ten feet away.

"You are not blind," the boy said. "You're looking right at me through those sunglasses."

"Okay, so I'm not blind. I just see things differently."

"Here, catch." The boy tossed the hardball he must have picked up.

Jon's hands went out, but the ball hit him on the chest and rolled along his arms, which were held close together in front of him. Finally he grasped the ball.

The boy walked up to Jon. "If you're really blind, how come you don't have one of those canes or a Seeing Eye dog?"

"You can't get a Seeing Eye dog until you're eighteen, and I'm ten."

"Me, too. But what about a cane?"

"I don't use it to come here because I know the way. I live over there, in that old white house next to the park."

"How do you know it's white?"

"That's what sighted people call it."

"Did you just move in?"

"Hey, Matt," a kid called from the playing field, "we're waiting for the ball."

"I'd better go."

"Here, catch," Jon said, throwing the ball right to Matt. "See you later."

"Yeah, see you later."

Again Jon faced the bay at the edge of the park and felt the end-of-summer breeze tousle his brown hair. The water lapped gently against the land and left no sharp line between what was dry and what was wet. In more places than not, there was mud that Jon knew he'd feel under the grass if he walked too close to the water.

He had lived here in Kellam's Landing long ago, before the car accident. He was only two when that had happened, and he didn't remember the time when he could see. He didn't remember his father, who had died in the accident. He didn't remember that his mother had sung to him, as Grandma said she had.

Before the accident, they had moved close to Washington, D.C. His father had gotten a good job there, his mother first told Jon when he was old enough to understand. "But Daddy wasn't happy," she said. "At night after work, he would sit and carve shore birds. He had never bothered much with carving but in that apartment five floors up, he began to think about Kellam's Landing and the mushy marshes and the silent ponds where ducks and birds made their nests." They decided that when they had saved some money, they would go home again, to where people knew one another. They'd open up a shop where they could sell the carvings and other shore things. That had been the plan until the accident on the Beltway.

Jon had heard the story many times. "You were on your way back from the zoo with your daddy," Jon's mother would start. "He liked to go there with just you. Then a tractor-trailer driven by a drunk cut over from another lane."

The story always ended at that point because Jon's mother couldn't talk about it any longer. After a while, Jon had stopped asking about the accident. He never heard anything new, and it only made his mother cry.

Jon didn't remember his operations or much about the long hospital stays, except that while he was there he played with his father's carvings. His mother would say, "This is the bufflehead. This is the ruddy duck," and she would move Jon's hands all over each one. Pretty soon he knew the difference between one diving duck and another, even though he'd never be able to see them.

Now, after going to a special school near Washington, Jon was back in Kellam's Landing, where he had been born. "You can go to public school," his mother had said, "back home."

But Jon didn't think of this as home yet. For now they were living with Grandma in her house next to Bayside Park. Even though they had come here to visit many times, home was still the apartment near Washington, with all the city sounds just outside.

Jon was worried about going to public school, too. He'd be the only blind person there. Most of the kids at the special school he had gone to were blind or had a visual handicap. Even the principal was blind. She'd say, "We just see things differently. Don't be afraid to try something new because of it." But after what had happened in the park with that kid, Matt, Jon knew that being in a place where nobody else was blind would be a lot different from what he was used to.

He turned toward Grandma's house and started walking along the edge of the gravel path that led to the sidewalk on Maple Street. Grandma's picket fence began there, just to the left, where the road curved around and followed the shape of the bay. Jon had learned the way fast enough. That was the easy part. But when would he really feel at home?

T wo

After supper Jon went upstairs to his room. It was in the back of the house and faced east, so at night it was cool there, with the sun ready to set in the western sky on the other side of the house. Jon stood at the open window. In Washington they had been near a corner with a traffic light. From his room there, Jon could tell when the light turned by the sounds that vehicles made as they started and stopped. On the windows there were miniblinds that rattled when the breeze blew.

Here the soft cotton curtains brushed the sill, and the shade flapped against the raised glass pane. Way out back, past the marsh, a flock of geese flew up and away from the quiet water as a fishing boat came home with its motor softly humming. Jon liked listening to these evening sounds. But now it was time to work on his typing.

He had practiced all summer and was getting pretty good at it. There were two more weeks before school started, and his new teacher had said he must learn to type so he could do the written work. He couldn't exactly turn in braille to a sighted teacher.

Jon thought about his new teacher. He and his mother had met her at the end of the last school year, before they had moved.

"You know, Jon," she had said to him, "I didn't really want you to be in my class. There are two sixth grade teachers, but I'm the one with more experience. We'll do the best we can. Won't we?"

He had said he would, but he disliked her already.

"You'll sit off to the side," she had told him. "That way you won't distract the rest of the class with all the special material you'll use."

Jon's mother had said that maybe the woman just needed a vacation. "You'll be able to do whatever the other kids do for schoolwork," she had assured him. "When she sees that, everything will be fine. Besides, the law says you have a right to go to that public school, like everyone else."

Jon put some paper in the typewriter and then started playing the typing book that was recorded on cassettes. He moved his fingers easily as the woman's voice on the tape directed him to press each key: ASDF JKL; FG FG FG FG JH JH JH JH. The hard part was typing sentences as they were spoken. That was on another tape. But Jon didn't feel like doing that tonight, even though he was getting better at it.

When he was about halfway through the first tape, he heard a knock on his door. He could tell it was his mother, one loud and one soft rap.

"You have a visitor," she said. "Matt's here." Then she left.

The boy at the park, Jon thought. "Come on in." He got up and turned off the cassette player.

"What were you doing?" Matt asked.

"I have to learn to type so I can do written work for school."

"What grade are you going into?"

"Sixth."

"Me, too. Maybe we'll be in the same class. There are

two sixth grades. One of the teachers is really nice. She was new last year, Mrs. Lester. The other one is a crab, Mrs. Grayson. We call her Mrs. Gruesome."

"I have her," Jon said.

"I hate the way she looks."

"I don't know about that, but her voice was kind of high and shrill when we met her, sort of like the wicked witch in the *Wizard of Oz*. She doesn't want me in her class because I'm blind."

"Mrs. Grayson is mean to everyone, and I shouldn't have talked to you the way I did this afternoon, either. That's what I came over to say."

"That's okay. Do you want to play cards?"

"Sure."

Jon took a deck from his desk drawer. "We can play on the rug. Is gin rummy okay?"

"Hey, wait a minute," Matt said. "How can you tell what the cards are?"

"See these little dots in the corner? They're braille. All I have to do is touch them and I know what number and suit the card is."

"How do you know I won't cheat and look at your cards while we're playing?"

Jon laughed. "How do you know I won't feel the braille dots on your cards while I'm dealing?"

"We're even," Matt said. "I never saw cards with braille on them."

"My mother typed them on with a braillewriter."

"What's that?"

"It's on the table near the typewriter. It has six keys for punching braille dots. I started learning to use it in first grade, just like you learned to write."

"Can you type my name with it?" Matt said.

"Don't you want to play cards?"

"First type my name."

Jon took a piece of heavy paper and put it into the braillewriter. "How do you spell it?"

"M-a-t-t-h-e-w N-o-t-t-i-n-g-h-a-m."

When Jon had finished, he checked it with his fingers, took the paper out, and gave it to Matt. "I'll still use the braillewriter when school starts, but I'll have to retype everything on the regular typewriter for Mrs. Gruesome to read."

"Will you teach me braille and show me how to type on a braillewriter someday?" Matt said. "It'll be like learning a secret code that none of the kids here know."

"If you want." Except for those in his swimming class at the Y, all of Jon's friends before this had been blind. Jon sat on the rug again and started shuffling the cards.

"Wait," Matt said, walking to the bookshelves. "Where did you get all these carvings?"

"My dad did them, but he's dead." Jon put the cards in his pocket and went over to the shelves. He picked up a carving of a plover and felt it lovingly. "Go ahead. You can pick them up, too."

"There's an old carver who lives next door to me," Matt said after a while. "He's supposed to be one of the best on the whole shore. But he sits under a big tree next to his house and never looks up from his carving except to yell at us to get away."

"How come?"

"My mom says he didn't used to be that way before his wife died, but I don't remember him when he was nice."

"Sort of like my mother not singing after my father died." Jon turned away from the shelves and took out the cards. Someday he was going to learn how to carve. He had decided that when his mother told him they were moving back to Kellam's Landing.

"It's getting dark," Matt said. "I think I'd better go home, or else I'll get yelled at. What are you doing tomorrow?"

"My mother's going to make me go shopping for school clothes late in the morning, after she gets through with work. She waitresses at Skipper's, and she's on breakfast shift this week. I could go bike riding in the afternoon."

"Oh, yeah? How are you going to do that?" Matt said.

"Come on. I'll show you."

They went downstairs and out to the garage. A bicycle built for two was leaning against a wall. Jon put his hands on the front handlebars. "My grandmother and grandfather used to ride it, and when I visited I could ride it, too, with someone in front steering."

Matt put his hands near Jon's on the front handlebars. "Do you think I could do that?"

"Why not?" Then he said, "You'd better go, or you'll get yelled at."

"I'll see you tomorrow," Matt said.

"See you," Jon answered.

T H R E E

THE SMELL OF MUFFINS AND BACON DRIFT-
ED UPSTAIRS and awoke Jon, making him hungry.
Grandma believed in big breakfasts. "It gives you a
good start in the day," she'd say, sounding just like a
breakfast cereal commercial.

When she heard Jon come into the kitchen, she said,
"I was just going to wake you. Do you want eggs?"

"Sure, and you made bacon?"

"Yes, I did. Just took the cornmeal muffins out of the
oven, too," Grandma said. "Will you loosen them from
the tin, Jon?"

"How come you don't use those little paper hold-
ers?"

"Your grandpa didn't like them. He said half the muffin stuck to the paper when you pulled it off. It didn't really, but I decided not to fuss about it. Still don't use them, even though he's gone. I guess habits die hard." She spilled the beaten eggs into the frying pan with a sizzling sound.

Jon got a dull knife and started loosening the muffins. They were still hot and would melt the margarine he'd put on them.

"Hey, Grandma, promise you won't yell?"

"Why, what did you do wrong?"

"Nothing, but I want to do something and I think it would upset Mom."

"Then don't do it." She scraped the scrambled eggs and bacon onto Jon's plate. "Help yourself to muffins. The eggs are at nine o'clock and the bacon is at three."

"You don't have to tell me that. There aren't so many foods there." Grandma liked to compare the plate to a clock.

"Now, what do you have in mind to do?" She pulled a chair out from the table and sat down, too.

"I want to learn how to carve," Jon said.

There was silence.

"Grandma?"

She sighed. "You've got to try everything, don't you." There was more tenderness than disapproval in her voice. "You have to learn how to use a knife, a sharp one that you could cut yourself with."

"I've cut some vegetables and bread with a sharp knife, and I have a pocketknife."

"I've never seen you with that." She sounded alarmed.

"I found it in Bayside Park, stepped right on it. Nobody was around to claim it."

"You're right about your mom being upset if you started carving," Grandma said.

"But why?"

"She still hasn't put some feelings in the memory box. She carries them around with her every day."

"What are you talking about?"

"Your mother could remember with love what happened when your father was alive, but she remembers with pain. I told you she used to sing while he was alive. She can't sing now, because she's still hurting from what happened."

"But she wants me to do whatever else I can do. She

doesn't say don't ride the bike or don't go to school with sighted kids."

"This has nothing to do with your being blind, Jon. It has to do with the fact that if you start carving, it will bring back memories she's not able to deal with, the memories she has of your father carving."

"If I start carving, will you tell her?"

"Now, Jon, you're putting me in a hard position. If I don't know you're carving, then it will be easier for me."

Jon got up from his chair and hugged her. "Thanks, Grandma."

"If you decide to do it, find someone good to teach you, but leave me out of it."

"I already have someone I want to learn from."

"Who?"

"I'm not telling you, remember?"

Grandma laughed. "Go upstairs and make your bed. Your mother will be home soon enough to take you clothes shopping for school, and you'd better be ready."

"I wish I didn't have to be in Mrs. Grayson's class."

"She wasn't very pleasant when you met her."

"Matt said she's mean to everyone."

"Then you can't take it personally. Think of it as her problem. She was always rather difficult."

"Do you know her, Grandma?"

"This is a small town, Jon. It's not easy to hide."

"What do you mean?"

"Everyone knows the good and bad of folk. And most times, we accept one another. Most times there's some good in any person. Maybe you just have to look harder for it in Mrs. Grayson."

That afternoon, Matt came over around two o'clock. Jon was waiting for him in the driveway with the bicycle. He had oiled it and wiped the gritty dirt off the frame, so it was ready to go.

"I'm not sure I can ride one of these things," Matt said, rolling it along the driveway. "I want to be in front."

"No kidding!"

But once they both got on the bicycle, it was easy. They went down Maple and turned onto Lincoln.

"Warn me when a stop sign is coming," Jon said. "There's not enough traffic for me to tell."

After they had ridden for a while, Matt asked, "Do

you want to go to my house? We can get something to drink."

"Okay."

"We have to take the next right, just ahead."

"I hear ducks," Jon said.

"There's a pond in back of the houses on my side of the street."

The boys rounded the corner.

"Carver's out," Matt whispered, "sitting with his cat under the tree."

The boys rode by quickly and turned into Matt's driveway, just past Carver's house.

"Is he carving?"

"Yes."

"What's his real name?"

"Lewis is his last name, but I don't know his first. It's something like Elmer or Everett or Emmett. Everyone just calls him Carver."

"Do you have anything he made?"

"Are you kidding? Each duck he carves sells for more than a thousand dollars. That's way more than other carvers get around here at shows or at shops. People say he's rich, but he sure doesn't look it with his old clothes and hair that always flys out wild."

"Do you think he'd teach me how to carve?"

"He'd probably start yelling and say something mean about your being blind. Why do you have to carve? You can't see."

"Is that what he'd say to me?"

"I don't know," Matt said. "I'm sorry." He put his hand on Jon's shoulder. "Let's just go in and get something to drink. You probably won't have any trouble with Carver."

Jon wondered about that. First his new teacher didn't want him in her class. Now Matt just about said he shouldn't try carving because he was blind. How would Carver act toward him? Jon knew that somehow he'd find a way to meet him. He'd ask Carver to teach him, too. Maybe, just maybe, Carver would agree.

F OUR

MATT SAID HE WOULD HELP, so for the next week plenty of spying went on. Sometimes, first thing in the morning, the two of them would hear Carver running the band saw, doing some rough cutting. After that he might come out and walk to the pond behind the houses to watch the ducks. A few would let him pick them up and hold them for a little while. In the afternoon, he'd sit under the big tree next to his house and carve with his cat lying near him.

But another week went by, and there didn't seem to be a right time to go up to Carver. Pretty soon the weather would turn colder and he'd start working inside.

"I'm getting tired of watching him and telling you everything he does," Matt said as they got off Jon's bike in front of Waverly's Drugstore. "Maybe the only reason you want to be with me is so you can meet Carver."

"That's not true. I came here so you could get school supplies, and I'm teaching you how to use the braille-writer."

"There are other carvers you can learn from," Matt said, "and they're nicer."

"He's the best. You told me that."

"Then just go up and ask him if he'll teach you. I'm not spying anymore. School starts tomorrow, and after I get a notebook and some paper, I'm going to play baseball."

They went inside the drugstore, and Jon held Matt's arm above the elbow, following him down an aisle toward the school supplies. There were other people there, but none of the voices were familiar to Jon.

All of a sudden, Matt stopped. "There's Carver," he whispered, "talking to someone I don't know."

"Can we get closer without them seeing us?"

"We'll turn right in a couple of feet and then left down the next aisle."

The boys listened.

"I need a reference," Carver said. "A blue-winged teal drake. I did the hen for a man in Baltimore, and now he wants the mate."

"Season is the beginning of October," the other man answered. "It's over three weeks away, so you'll have to wait. You know that. But I'll see what I can do then."

Jon stood close to Matt. "What are they talking about?"

"I'll tell you outside," Matt whispered. "I thought you'd know about references. You should if you want to carve."

As they rode the bike away from the store, Matt explained. "When you live here, you know about carving and hunting because they're things so many people do. A reference is what you use for a model. Some carvers hunt and save the skins so they'll know how to make the feathers just the right colors and shapes. Carver must get his references from other people."

"If I could bring him a blue-winged teal drake, he'd at least talk to me," Jon said.

"My father hunts."

"Could he get me a teal this season?"

"I'll ask, but it's never a sure thing. He might not be lucky."

"Did you ever go hunting?" Jon asked.

"A couple of times, but I didn't like it. Eating the ducks afterward was even worse. My father says duck hunting is in his blood, since my grandpa was a market hunter."

"What's that?"

"He sold what he killed to food stores."

That night, while Jon was practicing his typing, his mother came up to his room. "Mrs. Grayson called today," she said.

Jon stopped. "Why?"

"One of your books hasn't come in yet, a math book that she wanted transcribed into braille."

"When will it be ready?"

"She didn't know and was a bit upset. I told her you'd learn fine by listening, and I'd help you at night."

"We should have stayed in Washington," Jon said.

"Maybe Mrs. Grayson is just afraid."

"Afraid of what?"

"Afraid of teaching someone who learns in a different way."

"Teachers aren't afraid," Jon said.

"Everybody's afraid sometimes."

"I guess so." He thought about wanting Carver to teach him and how there hadn't seemed to be a good time to ask him right out. Maybe he wasn't just waiting to give Carver the blue-winged teal. Maybe he was afraid.

The math book came in during the second week of school, and Mrs. Grayson called Jon up to her desk. "I don't know how they expect me to understand this, but as long as you hand in your assignments typewritten and pass the tests, you can stay in my class. So far you're doing fine, and I didn't think you would. Of course that braillewriter is a distraction, but I guess we'll have to put up with the noise."

Jon thanked her for the book and took it to his seat. He was getting along fine with the other kids, so it no longer mattered as much what Mrs. Grayson said to him. But now, more than ever, he wanted to learn how to carve—and not only for himself. He had to show Mrs. Grayson he could do something she'd never believe he could do.

Before hunting season started, Jon decided to learn something about the blue-winged teal. If Matt's father got one for him to take to Carver, Jon didn't want to say anything stupid. He and Matt took a wildlife book from the library.

" 'Teals are dabblers,' " Matt read out loud as they sat on the rug in Jon's room one afternoon. " 'They are freshwater birds, and when they feed they tip their tails up and stick their heads in the water as they dabble for food.' "

"Where do you hunt them here?" Jon asked.

"My dad goes to Kellam's Pond or to the swales that fill up with rainwater near the marshes."

"What are swales?"

"Low spots."

Jon went over to the shelf where he kept his father's carving of a blue-winged teal. He picked it up, as he had every day lately, and ran his fingers along the narrow neck. He felt the high side pockets, where feathers covering the wings rested against the body. He touched the long head, which the book said was shaped almost like a teardrop.

But Jon wasn't prepared for the way the real duck felt. A couple of weeks later, on the first day of hunting season, Matt's father handed him one. It lay limp in his open palms as Matt's father walked away.

"Feel its bones," he said to Matt.

"I know, and carvings don't have bones."

Jon put the dead teal on the cement near Matt's back door and touched its short, hairlike breast feathers. Then he moved his hands along its back to the tail feathers. The October air was cool, even with the sun shining. Jon shivered a little.

"I'm going to take it over to Carver now," he said firmly.

"What are you going to say to him?"

"I don't know yet. Do you have a bag I can put the teal in?"

A few minutes later, Jon was walking over to Carver's house with the paper bag in one hand and his cane in the other, sweeping it in front of him from side to side to warn him of obstacles. Matt had said that Carver was inside. There was a front porch on his house with steps leading up to it. Maybe he wouldn't even answer the door. No matter what, Jon knew he wasn't going to turn around now.

F IVE

JUST AS JON WAS ABOUT TO RING THE
BELL, he felt Carver's cat rub against his right leg. This
surprised him, and he jumped. The cat meowed and
moved away.

Jon pressed the doorbell button, but no sound came
from the box inside the house. He rapped on the door,
and the cat rubbed up against him again. This time Jon
stooped down to pet it. But with the sound of footsteps
coming closer to the door, Jon straightened up fast.

The door opened after a few tugs to loosen it where
its wood must have swelled and stuck to the frame.
Carver spoke gruffly. "I'm not interested in giving to
charities," he said. And he slammed the door shut.

Jon knocked again.

"I told you," Carver yelled from behind the closed door, "no charities, not for the blind or anyone else."

It was the cane, Jon thought. "I'm not collecting for charities," he called out. "I have something for you."

"What do you have?"

"A blue-winged teal drake."

Carver opened the door again. He took the bag from Jon and opened it. "Well, I'll be. First day of the season." Then, in a suspicious voice, he asked, "Where did you get this?"

"Matt's father shot it."

"Who's that?"

"They live next door to you," Jon said.

"How do you know I want this?"

"Me and Matt heard you say you did one day in Waverly's."

"Matt and I," Carver yelled back. Then, more quietly, he asked, "Do you live around here?"

"Me and my—" Then he corrected himself. "My mother and I live with my grandma."

"Who's that?"

"Evelyn Mears."

"Evie Mears." Carver's voice was gentle. Then he cleared his throat. "I went to school with her. What's your name?"

"Jon Bailey." The cat rubbed against Jon again, then lay down across his feet.

"I can't pay you. It's against the law to sell migratory wildfowl," Carver said. "Go ahead and pet him. He likes you."

Jon squatted. He rubbed the cat's belly and felt the fine fur behind its ears. The other cats he had touched in Kellam's Landing had coarse fur. Then Jon stood up again and said, "I don't expect pay, but would you teach me how to carve?"

"You want to carve?"

"Yes."

"Have you ever done it before?"

"No."

"Why do you want to learn?"

Jon told him about his father's carvings. "I hold them and I want to be able to do it, too."

"You have to know how to use a knife."

"I know."

"Come down the steps with me," Carver said. The

cat followed them. "Tell me about Chips."

"What do you mean?"

"My cat. Is he fat? Is he skinny? Tell me about him."

"Why?"

"Don't do it. See if I care."

Jon folded his cane and put it in his pocket. He reached for the cat, which walked back and forth, rubbing against his legs, not seeming to notice the cross-sounding conversation. When Jon started touching him, the cat stopped pacing. Gently, Jon let his fingers trace the outline of the cat's pointed ears, then opened his hands to hold the animal's body, telling Carver what he knew about the cat as he learned it.

"Should I pick him up?"

"What do you think?"

Jon lifted the cat and brought him against his body until the back legs rested on Jon's forearm and the front legs rested on Jon's shoulder. Jon talked about where the legs were attached to the body and the feel of the paw pads and claws.

"You have good hands," Carver said. "You can feel shapes, and that's the important thing. These young carvers see colors. They see sets of feathers, but they don't always get the shape right. Now, you listen to me. If you're going to be afraid, don't you come back."

"You mean you're going to teach me?"

"I'm not giving you any special treatment. Now go home and learn about cutting carrots with a good sharp paring knife."

"Carrots?"

"You heard me. You're not deaf, too, are you?"

Jon smiled. "When should I come back?"

"When do you think?"

"When I've learned about cutting carrots."

"You'd better keep some Band-Aids handy." Carver laughed as he went up the steps and inside.

Jon went back to Matt's house, and they walked down to the pond in back to talk in private.

"I tried to listen from my bedroom window," Matt said, "but I couldn't hear. I was wondering why you spent so much time playing with the cat."

"He wanted to see if I noticed shapes. He said getting the right shape is the important thing in carving. Then he told me to go learn how to cut carrots."

That evening, before supper, Jon went into the kitchen. His mother and grandmother were there.

"What are we having?" he asked them.

"Roast chicken, mashed potatoes, and green beans," his mother answered.

"What about a salad?"

"I thought you didn't like salads," she said.

"I'll help make it," Jon said.

Grandma laughed. "That's too good an offer to turn down. There's lettuce and tomatoes in the left vegetable crisper. Take out the half of a pepper and a carrot, too. I'll help with the cutting."

"I can do it. Just give me a knife."

Jon saved the carrot for last. He had never cut one before. "First peel it," his mother said, handing him the peeler she had just finished using. "I do it away from me."

"I'd rather do it toward me," Jon said.

"Suit yourself."

When he'd finished peeling the carrot, Jon picked up the paring knife. At first it went in easily. Then it hit a hard part. Jon wiggled the carrot, urging the knife through, toward his thumb. The cutting sound was changing. When the knife blade hit Jon's thumb pad lightly, one carrot slice dropped onto a plate. He put the sharp edge of the knife against the carrot, ready to cut it again. If Carver said learn to cut carrots, that's what he would do.

S I X

ON SATURDAY MORNING, Jon had his mother drop him off at Matt's house. That way she wouldn't know he was really planning on going to Carver's.

"He's out back at the pond," Matt said when he met Jon outside. "I have to clean my room. When you're done with him, come over."

Jon walked confidently to the pond, counting his steps, knowing it would take about fifty to get there. As he got closer, he heard Carver talking quietly to the ducks, which fluttered their wings softly as they flew up, then down quickly. Their quacking was more like conversation than sounds of alarm. Jon had been there often enough with Matt, so the ducks didn't startle at his presence. It was Carver who spoke first.

"You came back," he said.

"I learned how to cut carrots."

Carver laughed. "Is that so? How do you cut carrots?"

Jon told him. "But I don't want to cut any more. I'm tired of eating them."

"So you use your thumb as a guide. That's called leverage. Come here."

Jon walked toward Carver. "Now I'm going to pick up this mallard," Carver said. "I know him, and I want you to get to know him."

Jon touched the duck, which was held firmly in Carver's hands. "His head is low. Between his shoulders."

"That's because he's relaxed. Stroke his back. Feel the cape feathers right behind the head. They cover the shoulder feathers near the sides of the neck, just like a cape. Do you know what a cape is?"

"It's like a coat without sleeves," Jon said.

"Now the scapulars," Carver went on. "They start out shorter near the cape area and get longer as they

go toward the tertials. The flight feathers stick out under them. All the feathers flow from head to tail."

Jon moved his hand slowly toward the duck's tail, feeling all the feather groups. "They overlap."

"Like roof shingles," Carver said. "Now sit down. I want you to hold the duck."

Jon moved his feet around, feeling the ground where Carver told him to sit.

"You afraid of something?" Carver said, annoyed.

"I don't want to sit in duck droppings."

"Then sit back on the grass a bit and stop fussing about."

Jon sat down, and Carver handed him the mallard. The duck stayed put while Carver directed Jon. "Feel the side pockets. You know what side pockets are, don't you?"

"The feathers covering the wings when they're close to the body."

"Right. Are they high or low?"

"Low."

"On both sides?"

"Yes."

"What does that mean?" Carver said fast.

"The duck is even."

"Even!" Carver shouted. "Don't they teach you vocabulary in school?"

Jon didn't answer. He let go of the duck, and it flew off when he started to get up. "What's wrong with *even?*"

"The word is *symmetrical,*" Carver said. "What's generally true of one side of the body is true of the other side, too. Now, on any one duck there might be slight differences, just the way people can have one foot a little bigger than the other."

"When am I going to start carving?" Jon asked, discouraged.

"Follow me."

"Where are you going?"

"To my garage." Carver started walking away and then stopped. "Aren't you coming?"

"If I hold onto your arm, it will be easier." He didn't want to have to explain.

Carver came back. "You have to show me what to do," he muttered.

The garage smelled of wood, a wood smell that reminded Jon of something else. In a minute he knew what it was. His grandmother had a storage closet in the attic that was lined with cedar. This was like that smell, only not as strong.

"Is there a lot of wood here?" he asked.

"Half a tree trunk. It's Atlantic white cedar, the best wood for working decoys. It doesn't rot in water." He picked up a chunk and handed it to Jon.

Jon smelled the piece in his hand. "My grandmother has a cedar closet."

"Tennessee aromatic cedar, probably. That's what they make them out of. It's stronger smelling and harder. This wood came from the New Jersey Pine Barrens. It grew near a stream the color of tea. But you wouldn't know about that, would you."

"How'd you get it?"

"What do you care for?" Then Carver said, "You need a good knife."

"I have one." Jon showed Carver the pocketknife he had in his jeans.

"Not like that. How do you expect to carve without the right knives?"

"I'll get one."

"One? You need different ones for different jobs."

"How much do they cost?"

"Too much."

Jon stood silent and then offered the wood he was holding to Carver. "I'd better go."

Carver breathed deeply. "If I let you take one of my knives . . ." He paused. "I'll want to get it back," he said sharply.

"I'll give it back."

Carver put a round, thick knife handle into Jon's hand. The blade was wide and flat, tapering to a point at the end. It was sharpened on one long edge. Jon held it, curving his fingers into a fist around the handle. Then he felt the blade carefully. "It's sharp."

"What did you expect? I'll give you a box to put it in. Then, go."

"Aren't you going to teach me how to use it?"

"I don't have all day. You've got to figure that out yourself."

As Jon was about to leave, Carver said, "You coming back next Saturday?"

"Should I?"

"Don't you want to learn how to carve?"

Jon smiled. "What time should I come?"

"About nine."

"I'll be here."

"You'd better be. You have my knife. Take this wood, too," Carver said, handing Jon back the piece of cedar. Then Jon heard Carver go into the house, slamming the door shut.

S E V E N

THE PARK WAS THE BEST PLACE TO PRAC-
TICE till the weather turned really cold. There wouldn't
be any wood shavings around for Jon's mother and
grandmother to see. He could concentrate on carving
instead of worrying about getting caught. Sometimes
Matt came with him after school.

"What will you do if your mom finds out?" Matt
asked as he watched Jon one afternoon.

"How will she find out?"

"My mother always finds out when I do something
I shouldn't do. One time she dropped me off at the
library and I went to meet some kids at the arcade. I
was going to be back at the library in time to be picked

up, but she walked into the arcade an hour earlier. 'Time to go,' she said, and we all followed her out, without even finishing our games. It was sort of like one of those police raids you see on TV. She took all of us home and never would tell me how she found out where we were."

Jon made a shallow cut and felt a thin shaving curl off the cedar and onto his lap. "I think my mother will try to make me stop if she finds out now."

"She doesn't mind you using knives in the kitchen?"

"I told you, it's because she can't handle me doing what my father loved to do."

"Is that why you want to do it?"

"Lots of people here carve. Why shouldn't I?"

"Because you're blind."

"So what. You feel sorry for me, don't you?"

"No. I just don't think of a blind person doing something like carving."

"Don't think of me as different," Jon said angrily. "I'm going to carve if I want to. I like doing it, and I'm going to keep doing it till I'm really good at it, like anyone who can see." As he talked, he cut into the wood faster and faster. Then the knife slipped. The

50

long edge hit his thumb too hard, and he dropped the knife.

Matt picked it up. "Are you okay?"

"What difference does it make?" Jon felt the blood ooze out of the cut.

"Come on, you've got to take care of it," Matt said.

"I'm not going to stop carving just because of this."

"Are you going to stop if your mother finds out?"

"Not now."

"I didn't think so."

The next Saturday, Carver was outside when Jon got to his house. Jon heard him whack at some wood under the tree.

"What are you doing?"

"Do you have my knife?" Carver asked, not answering the question.

"It's in my backpack." Jon took out the box and held it toward him.

Carver stopped. "Are you done with it?"

"No."

"Then don't give it to me," he snapped.

Jon pulled back his hand.

"I'm just sitting here," Carver said, finally answering

the question, "balancing a rough-cut duck body on an old stump and whacking off slices of wood with a hatchet. What did you learn about carving this week?"

Jon took out the wood and showed Carver. "I'd rather cut toward my thumb than away from it. Then I know where the knife is."

Carver laughed. "I can see that. What did your mother say?"

Jon felt the Band-Aid. "Nothing. She didn't notice." He didn't want to tell Carver he had made up a lie about it. "I got mad at someone while I was carving. Now I know you don't do that."

"Are you mad now?"

"No."

Carver handed a file and sandpaper to Jon. "Smooth the wood out with these, and don't bother me. I don't want to whack my hand off."

An hour later, Jon said, "Am I done?"

"Why are you asking me?" But Carver stopped his whacking. "You should know by feeling it."

Jon ran his hand over it. "It's pretty good."

"Pretty good isn't good enough. Take it home and work on it. I brought another piece out for you, too.

Now I don't have any more time for talk."

Jon put the wood in his pack. "You don't mind if I use your knife again?"

"You'll bring it back, won't you?"

"Yes."

Carver rummaged through a box and handed Jon a knife with a curved blade. "Here. Take this, too. It's good for rounding out shapes, making contours. Keep it with the straight blade."

Jon zipped up his pack. "I'll be back next Saturday."

"Unless your mother is afraid you'll cut your fingers off." Carver laughed and started whacking the wood with his hatchet again.

Jon headed toward Matt's house. If only Carver knew it was a secret. A cloud must have covered the sun, for the October air suddenly felt cooler. Jon would have to carve inside soon. Maybe Matt could help him figure out a way. Really, he knew himself what he'd have to do. Keeping it a secret would just make him tell more lies. He'd have to tell his mother about his carving. But he had to find the right time.

E IGHT

WHILE MATT TYPED ON THE BRAILLE-
WRITER, Jon carved. He let the shavings fall onto newspaper that was spread on the floor of his room. That
was Matt's idea. It worked, since the shavings could
be wrapped in the newspaper and taken out to the
garbage pail when nobody was around. It was already
November and too cold to carve outside.

Matt stopped typing. "Maybe if your mother saw
something you made, she wouldn't get upset."

"Maybe, but I haven't made anything yet. I've just
been getting used to the knives." He felt the piece of
wood in his hand. It was the third piece Carver had
given him, and it was full of hollows and curves Jon had

cut. Part of it was sanded, and part was rough.

"You know what?" Matt said.

"What?"

"Maybe you're afraid to start making a duck."

"Why should I be afraid?"

"Because you don't know if it will turn out right."

Jon didn't say anything.

"Maybe you don't want anyone to see you have trouble doing something. You didn't like my seeing you get cut. Sighted people get cut, too, you know."

"I'll be able to carve ducks."

"Then why don't you do it?"

Jon was silent. Then he said, "I don't just want to carve to prove something."

"I know."

The next Saturday morning, Jon walked up Carver's front steps and knocked hard on the door. Carver opened it easily.

"You fixed it," Jon said, noticing that the door didn't stick anymore.

"The cool weather did some good, and I planed it," Carver said.

Jon went in and put down his pack on the gritty

floor. Then he took out his wood and the knives. Now that the weather was cold, Carver worked in the living room. There was a long table under a side window where he painted his carvings.

"The blue-winged teal drake is nearly done," Carver said. "I keep the skin of the reference bird right next to it while I work." He sat down in his big easy chair near the front window. Jon knew it must be covered with shavings and wood dust, since Carver sat there as he fine-carved and sanded.

"I'm ready to make a duck," Jon said, facing Carver.

"I was waiting for you to say that."

"You mean I could have started sooner?"

"No. You didn't think you were ready, and if you don't think you're ready, then you're not. It's all a matter of attitude. Nobody can tell you when it's the right time to do something, like me fixing the door." Carver laughed loudly at himself.

Jon didn't tell Carver what Matt had said. But it wasn't because of Matt that he wanted to make a duck. He knew he was ready.

Carver walked over to the shelves where he kept his finished birds and ducks. He took down a black duck and handed it to Jon. "What do you think?"

Jon felt the carving all over. "I think I can do it."

"I know you can. I'll rough cut the body with the band saw, and then you can get started."

They went out to the garage, and Jon listened as Carver moved around pieces of wood, looking for one without many knots. While Carver used the band saw, Jon thought about making his first duck. If it turned out well, he'd show it to his mother. He wanted her to know about his carving and feel happy about it. He'd show it to Mrs. Grayson, too.

"A blind boy, carving?" he imagined her saying.

"Why not?" he would answer boldly.

Back inside, Jon sat on the floor and worked, while Carver painted the teal. They didn't talk much till it was time for Jon to go. Usually that meant about one hour. Then Jon said, "My father made a black duck like this. I have it in my room."

"That's good," Carver said. "Then you won't be asking to borrow mine to use as a reference."

"How long will it take me to finish it?"

"How should I know? When do you want to have it finished?"

"By Thanksgiving."

"That's about three weeks."

At supper that night, Jon was quiet. He was thinking about the black duck.

"Is something wrong?" his mother said to him. "Is Mrs. Grayson giving you a hard time?"

"No. She's okay."

Jon thought of what had happened after school yesterday. He had had to go back to the classroom to pick up his homework. As he'd gone into the room, he'd heard someone using the braillewriter. Then the sound had stopped, and Mrs. Grayson had said, "Jon, did you forget something?" Her voice had come from where his desk was.

"Yes."

"I hope you don't mind my using your braillewriter."

"No."

"I'm learning." She had paused. "It's probably a waste of time."

"You could transcribe books into braille."

She had started to laugh and stopped short. "I could never do that." Then she had said, "You'd better hurry, or your bus will leave without you."

"Did you have a good time with Matt this morning?" Grandma asked, interrupting his thoughts.

"Yes."

"You've become good friends," his mother said, and then fell silent, too.

Maybe she already knew about his carving, Jon thought. He finished his supper quickly and asked to be excused. After he'd cleared his place, he went upstairs and closed the door behind him. Going over to the shelves where his father's carvings sat, he picked up the black duck. It was in a relaxed position, like Carver's. If only his carving could be good. Then he'd show it to his mother and hope she wouldn't be mad. He didn't like saying he was at Matt's house when he really wasn't. Maybe on Thanksgiving, Jon thought, he would have something to show her.

N I N E

JON SPENT EVERY SPARE MINUTE working on the duck. First he'd hold his father's black duck, moving his fingers along its curves. Then he'd pick up one of Carver's knives or the file and try to round his piece of cedar the same way. Sometimes Matt came to work on the braillewriter while Jon was carving, but mostly he carved alone now. He made sure no wood shavings were left on the floor. Just in case, he told his mother he'd vacuum his room. She didn't question him because she was used to Jon wanting to do things on his own.

Finally the body was finished, and the boys decided to put it in water to see how it would float. They went

out in back of Matt's house to the pond.

"Don't let it move away from us," Jon said as he kneeled and put the headless duck in the water.

"Don't worry. I can guide it back with your cane."

"How is it floating?" Jon asked.

"Kind of low."

"Carver said he'd hollow the inside out when I was ready for that. Then it will float right. Take it out now."

As they were walking back to Matt's house, Jon heard Carver's back door slam.

"What are you doing there?" he called to them.

"You talk to him," Matt said. "I'll meet you at my house."

"No, wait. He won't yell at you." Then Jon called out, "We were floating the body."

Carver laughed. "Who'd you kill?" He came up and took the duck's body from Jon. "Needs a head. Come on. I'll give you a rough one to work on. I just cut some on the saw."

The boys followed Carver into his garage. "I'm going to try out a few different heads, holding them in place on the duck's body." After a few minutes, he handed one to Jon. "This one's good. You'll have to carve it and make it fit. Then we'll glue it on."

"When will you hollow out the body?"

"Don't be impatient. You'll have it ready by Thanksgiving if that's really important to you."

That night, while Jon was working on fitting the head to the body, he felt the ridges of the grain on the body even though he had finished sanding it before putting it in the water. But now he took a piece of sandpaper and worked on it some more. Then he had an idea.

By the time he saw Carver again, Jon had dipped and sanded the carving till the wood felt like glass.

"How'd you get it so smooth?" Carver asked him.

"I brought out the grain by dipping it in water in the bathroom sink. After each dipping, I sanded it till there was no more to sand."

"It's good," Carver said quietly. "It's really good."

On the Saturday before Thanksgiving, the carving was all done. Instead of paint, Jon put dark rubbing oil on it. He did that at Carver's.

"You let it sit here to dry," Carver said. "I'll bring it over when I come for Thanksgiving dinner."

"You're coming for Thanksgiving dinner?"

"Evie asked me."

"Grandma?"

"You call her Grandma. I call her Evie."

"She didn't tell me."

"Did you tell her you were learning to carve?"

"Not exactly," Jon said quietly.

"So why should she tell you she asked me for Thanksgiving dinner? Don't you want me to come?"

Jon hesitated. "Sure I do."

"Doesn't sound that way."

"It's just that . . . Did you tell her you were teaching me to carve?"

"That's for you to tell."

Jon got up to go. "I think I'd rather show my mother the carving before you come. Would you give it to Matt to take to school for me the day before Thanksgiving?"

"Do you trust him with it?"

"He's my friend."

First thing Wednesday morning, Matt handed Jon a bag in the school yard. "I found a box, just the right size, with tissue paper in it."

"Do you think the duck looks all right?"

"Are you serious? It's better than any I've seen done by a kid and better than some I've seen done by grown-ups."

"While I was carving it, I thought about how I'd show it to Mrs. Grayson. I'd prove to her I could do something that she wouldn't think I could do. But now that I know I can do it, it doesn't matter what Mrs. Grayson thinks. Anyway, she's getting used to me, and I'm getting used to her. I guess someday she'll find out about my carving. But what do you think my mother will say?"

"If she doesn't like the duck, I'll take it."

"I'll make something for you next."

"A plover?"

"If you want. I hope she doesn't get mad."

Grandma was in the living room knitting when Jon walked in from school. He could hear the *click, click* of the needles and her favorite chair rocking back and forth. He sat down near her on the sofa.

"Carver said he's coming for Thanksgiving."

"Do you mean Emmett Lewis?"

"I guess that's his name. He lives next door to Matt."

"I went to school with him a long time ago,"

Grandma said, not breaking the rhythm of her knitting. "He was terribly bitter for a long time after his wife died, but I saw him last week at the supermarket and he was as nice as could be. Looked neater, too." Grandma paused. Then she said, "Poor man, he must be lonely. So I invited him for Thanksgiving dinner. That'll make nine of us with Aunt Sally and her family coming."

"He's been teaching me to carve, Grandma."

"I thought something was going on when you said you wanted to cut carrots. That's the sort of thing he'd say for you to do."

"You told me not to tell you if I wasn't going to tell Mom."

"Are you going to tell her now?"

"On Thanksgiving Day. I wanted to wait until I could show her something I made. If she sees what I can do, I think it will be all right."

"I think it will be all right, too. Now don't tell me any more. I want some surprise left."

On Thanksgiving Day everyone was up early. The turkey was in the oven at eight because dinner would be served at one. Jon had to set the table and help with the salad. His mother was peeling sweet potatoes for sweet potato biscuits, and Grandma was making pecan and pumpkin pies.

There didn't seem to be a really good time to show his mother the duck. But after he set the table, Jon decided not to wait any longer. He brought the box into the kitchen and went over to his mother. "I need to talk to you about something."

"Can't it wait?" she said. "There's a lot to do."

"You two go into the living room," Grandma said. "I can manage a few minutes without you."

Jon's mother put her arm around Jon as they left the kitchen. "Let's go sit down on the sofa."

"I've been keeping something a secret," Jon said, "because I thought you might get mad if I told you, and I didn't want to give up on it."

"What is it?" she asked, curious.

"I've been learning how to carve." Then Jon told his mother the whole story without stopping. "I didn't want to tell you until I could show you something I did." Jon handed his mother the box. "You can have this if you want it."

She lifted the cover off and took out the carving,

smooth as glass and shaped true to life. Jon heard her suck in her breath, but she didn't say anything.

"I used Dad's carving of a black duck as a model." He couldn't tell what she was thinking. Then she circled him with her arms, drawing him close. He felt tears running down her cheeks.

Finally she said, "It's beautiful, Jon. Your father would be very proud of you." Then she pulled away. "I'm proud of you, too."

"What would you have said if I had told you in the beginning that I wanted to learn to carve?"

"I think I would have said no because of painful memories I thought it would bring back." Then she paused. "But it wouldn't have been right. It wouldn't have been fair to you. Now I can see that your doing this brings back only the good memories. I'm glad you went ahead on your own. And today I'll have a chance to meet Carver."

"He's sort of different."

"He sounds like a very special person to me. Come. Let's show Grandma what you made."

A while after dinner, when everyone had left, Jon went upstairs to call Matt. He wanted to tell him what had happened. There would be no more secrets, and Carver was going to help him with a plover next. That would be for Matt. As Jon hung up the phone and started down the stairs, he heard singing coming from the kitchen. He sat down on a step and listened. It was his mother's voice, he could tell. The beautiful sound filled the house as if it had just discovered itself. Jon knew then that this was the best Thanksgiving he had ever had, and he felt right at home.

RUTH YAFFE RADIN

is the author of two other books for middle-grade readers, *Tac's Island* and *Tac's Turn*, as well as two picture books, *High in the Mountains*, illustrated by Ed Young, and *A Winter Place*, illustrated by Mattie Lou O'Kelley. She and her husband have three children and live in Bethlehem, Pennsylvania.

KARL SWANSON

has produced artwork for advertising and has illustrated numerous paperback and hardcover book jackets. This is his first illustrated book. Trained at the Art Students' League in New York City, he now lives with his wife in North Carolina.